The
Adirondack
Kids® #7

Mystery of the Missing Moose

By Justin & Gary VanRiper
Illustrations by Carol VanRiper

Adirondack Kids Press, Ltd.
Camden, New York

The Adirondack Kids® #7
Mystery of the Missing Moose

Justin & Gary VanRiper
Copyright © 2007. All rights reserved.

First Paperback Edition, March 2007
Second Paperback Edition, September 2008

Cover illustration by Susan Loeffler
Illustrated by Carol McCurn VanRiper

Photographs of moose, lynx and raccoon
© 2007 by Eric Dresser – www.nbnp.com

Published by
Adirondack Kids Press, Ltd.
39 Second Street
Camden, New York 13316
www.adirondackkids.com

Printed in the United States of America
by Patterson Printing, Michigan

ISBN 978-0-9707044-7-4

For Grandma & Grandpa VanRiper

Somehow there was always money for books

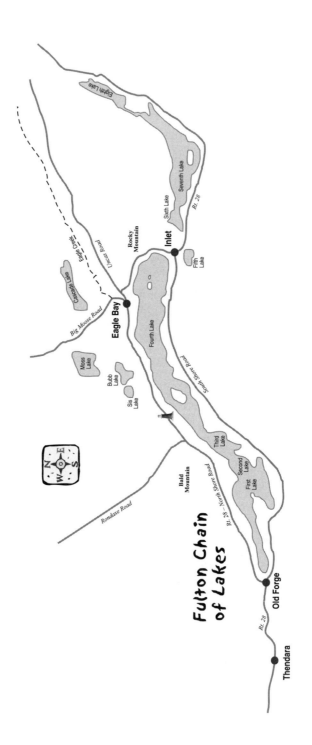

Fulton Chain
of Lakes

Contents

Justin crept to the edge of the yard and peered through the leaves into the forest. *see page 12*

Chapter One

Stir Crazy

"You're *bored*?" Justin Robert's mother did not want to hear it! "Find something to do," she said. "Work on the puzzle. Ride your bike. Go fishing." She handed him a copy of the *Weekly Adirondack* newspaper. "It's Friday. Maybe there is a new movie playing."

Justin held the newspaper in his hands and sighed while his mom returned to her work on the camp computer.

It had been a great summer – one of the most exciting ever. But how could she blame him for being bored? It was the middle of August and he had already caught the same six sunfish and three rock bass that hid under the dock at least a million times. He had even named them.

The sunfish that was missing one eye? That was *Cyclops*.

The smallest, thinnest sunny that took the bait every time? That was *Captain Hooked*.

And the meanest, darkest, greasiest rock bass that always fanned and stiffened its top fin, stabbing any poor fisherman who was unlucky enough to catch it, was named, *Stegosaurus*, like the dinosaur with the pointed plates on its back.

Justin's best friend, Nick Barnes, had always wanted to eat a rock bass to see what it tasted like, and every time *Stego* pricked Justin's tender palms, he was tempted to turn the nasty fish over to his hungry friend with french fries and a big bottle of ketchup.

Over the past seven summer weeks, Justin, along with Nick and another best friend, Jackie Salsberry, had investigated nearly every inch of Eagle Bay and Inlet. They had fished, hiked, sailed, kayaked, biked, shot arrows and, in Jackie's putt-putt, explored the vast waters of Fourth Lake motoring from island to island and shore to shore.

Even Justin's cat, Dax, was bored. Laying in the hot sun out on the porch floor, the sleek calico rolled onto her back, stretched and yawned. What else was there to do?

Justin joined his cat on the porch and slowly slid his short body back into an Adirondack chair. Mindlessly, he began thumbing through the newspaper, making sure he crinkled the pages loud enough so his mom would know he was reading it. He simply decided if he couldn't find anything to do *in* the paper, maybe he could at least make something *from* the paper – like fold it into a hat or a kite or a boat.

Thumbing through page after page, he looked at the pictures first and then skimmed the headlines of the short stories that explained what kinds of activities were happening in the area. Most of what he found was for adults and mainly involved sitting around. There were lectures and concerts, quilting and basket weaving.

Justin sighed again.

Dax yawned again.

"Stop it, Dax," said Justin. "You're going to make *me* yawn."

He was about to give up searching and start folding the paper into a kite, when a short headline in large bold type on the back page caught his attention.

Dax closed her eyes.

Justin's eyes opened wide. He jumped up and began moving frantically around the porch. Dax was so startled, she stood immediately, the hair on her back bristling.

"Where is my new camera, Mom?" Justin called out. Before she could answer, he found it sitting with his orange bucket hat alongside the partially-finished puzzle on the card table.

That stupid puzzle! he thought. Every summer his dad would pour out the pieces from a new jigsaw puzzle and then hide the box so no one would know what the picture looked like.

This year's camp puzzle had been especially tough. No one in the whole family was able to figure it out. They had found the four corners and put together most of the outside frame, but not much more. *What is it a picture of?* he wondered. The question was driving him crazy.

Justin glanced at the odd-shaped pieces that were

all organized in small piles according to their color. He slipped on his bucket hat and, to his surprise, found a blue piece that fit in the upper right-hand corner. A piece of the sky. Or was it water? Maybe they had the puzzle upside down. He snapped the piece in place and kept on moving.

Clutching the camera in one hand and the newspaper in the other, he called out to his mom again as he pushed with his shoulder to open the front screen door. "I'm going to Pioneer Village," he said, and bounded down the porch stairs. With Dax in swift pursuit, the door banged shut less than an inch from the end of her long, black tail.

Chapter Two

A Freaky Field Guide

"I'm not doing anything that even seems like school work," said Nick, with great resolve. "There's still a lot of summer left to go."

Justin entered the small community of stick houses and stores he and his friends had spent the summer building in the woods, and ran in the direction of Nick's voice. He guessed he was talking to Jackie. And he was right.

"I really don't care if you help or not," Jackie said to Nick. She shrugged. "I'm doing it anyway."

"Doing what?" asked Justin. He jumped up to join his friends on the large boulder, overlooking all of Pioneer Village, that had become their official meeting spot – *The Rock*.

Jackie ignored him, her steel-blue eyes still fixed on Nick. "Good," she said. "Now that Justin is here, we can vote on it."

"Vote on what?" asked Justin. "Will somebody tell me what's going on?"

Always overly dramatic, Nick waved his arms wildly in disgust. "She wants to teach summer school,"

"I really don't care if you help or not,"
Jackie said. "I'm making my field guide anyway."

he said. "Make us study and work and forget all about vacation."

Justin turned to Jackie. "Are you talking about your field guide again?"

"Yes, I am," said Jackie. "I'm going to make my book about all the mammals that live around our lake, even if I have to do it all by myself."

"I vote Jackie does her book all by herself," said Nick.

"Wait a minute," Jackie shot back. "That's not what we are voting on."

Justin held up his camera. "I vote we take a picture of a moose and make one hundred dollars," he said.

Both Jackie and Nick immediately stopped arguing and stared at him.

"Look at what I found in the newspaper," Justin said. He held up the back page of the paper to show them. Before they could see it, he turned the page back toward himself and started reading.

"Wanted," Justin began. "A good picture of the bull moose that was last seen on Main Street in Old Forge. The *Weekly Adirondack* will pay one hundred dollars for the best photograph of the moose sent in or dropped off at the office of the newspaper."

Jackie was happily surprised. "There is a moose around here? Great!" she said. "I never thought a moose would be one of the first animals in my field guide."

Nick was not so certain. "I'll bet somebody has already taken a picture of it and has the hundred dollars," he said.

7

"That's just it," said Justin. "The newspaper story says that the moose is missing. No one has seen it for a week. Not since it attacked and tore apart the stuffed bear on Main Street. After that, it just disappeared."

"I vote we search for the moose and Justin takes pictures for the *Fourth Lake Field Guide* of all the wild animals we see while we're looking," said Jackie.

"That's sneaky," said Nick. "We could just look for the moose and try to win the hundred dollars."

"I'll help if Dax can be in the field guide," said Justin. He reached out to his pet which had jumped up on *The Rock* right beside him.

"But Dax isn't a wild animal," Jackie said.

Justin shrugged. "Then I guess I can't help."

Jackie surrendered. "All right," she said. "Dax can be in the book."

"And I get to be in the field guide, too," said Nick.

Jackie turned her head toward him so fast it hurt her neck. "What?"

"And a newt," Nick added. "You have to put me in your field guide – and also a newt."

"But newts are amphibians," said Jackie. "No newts and no Nick Barnes."

"Then I vote, 'no'," Nick said.

Jackie shook her head in dismay. "All right. I'll put in the newt," she said. "But not you – I'm not adding one single *reptile*!"

"Then the vote is three to zero," said Justin with a smile. "Tomorrow we look for the missing moose."

Chapter Three

Picture Purrrrfect

"Hold still, Dax. Sit down." Justin was trying to take a photograph of his active feline friend for the field guide. But she was not cooperating at all.

"This is not why I got up at dawn," said Jackie. "I thought we were going to get an early start searching for the moose – not sit on the edge of your yard and watch you play with your cat."

Nick agreed. "Come on," he said, holding a pair of binoculars in his hands. "It feels like it's going to rain soon. Don't you have a billion pictures of Dax in your computer already?"

Every time Justin tried to press Dax's backside down to make her sit on the ground, she stood up on her hind legs and danced around.

Justin growled in frustration. "All the pictures I have of her are when she is running around on Captain Conall's mailboat or hanging out on the sleeping porch," he said, and continued to wrestle with his unruly model. "But I don't have any pictures of her looking like she is in the middle of the Adirondack forest. And I'm not stopping until I get a good one."

He picked her up and set her on the ground again, trying to ease her into the position he wanted. "Please sit down, Dax," he said. This time she went totally limp and rolled over on her back. Justin groaned.

"Let me try," said Nick. He set his binoculars down. "I'll give her some of my trail mix. Maybe that will make her sit up right."

"You have some trail mix?" said Jackie, surprised. "What kind? I like the fruit-and-nut mixes the best."

Nick reached into the pocket of his shorts, pulled out a small bag and shook it. "Let's see," he said, opening the bag. "There's m&ms, Good & Plenties and some Reese's Pieces."

"You call that trail mix?" Jackie asked.

"No," said Justin. "He calls that *breakfast!*"

"Here, Daxie," said Nick. He held a piece of candy out to her.

Dax sat up, and froze.

"Quick, take the picture," said Nick.

Jackie was stunned. "I can't believe it worked," she said.

The only thing that moved was Dax's head. She kept looking back over her shoulder. Otherwise she remained perfectly still. Justin snapped a picture. And then another. And another and another.

"Okay," said Jackie. "Isn't that enough?"

Justin shook his head and snapped a few more. "Dad says when he is taking pictures for magazines and books, he takes as many as he can because he never knows which one might come out just right.

Besides, she keeps turning her head." He snapped one more and stood up. "Okay, let's go find the moose."

"It's the weekend," Jackie said. "You know there will be a lot of tourists around."

Justin nodded knowingly. "That means there will also be lots of cameras to take a picture of the moose."

"Maybe that will be a good thing," said Nick. His friends looked at him curiously and he smiled. "Maybe the moose will keep hiding."

Justin shrugged and laughed. "Sure," he said. "There are plenty of places for a thousand pound moose to hide."

"Nick might be right," said Jackie. "Nobody has seen it lately. We have as good a chance as anybody to find it."

As the three friends prepared to head up the dirt driveway and out to Route 28 for the short walk to Eagle Bay, Dax still sat motionless.

"Is Dax going to help us on the search, or not?" asked Nick.

Justin frowned. "She's acting nervous," he said.

"She keeps looking over her shoulder toward the woods," said Nick.

"I knew she wasn't interested in your candy," said Jackie. "Dax senses danger." She grabbed Justin by the shoulder and whispered near his ear. "Let's find out what is scaring her," she said. "Your camera has a flash on it, right?"

Justin nodded.

Nick overheard her. "That's a good idea," he said

nervously, and picked up his binoculars. "You guys go ahead. I'd better wait here by the water pump, and make sure Dax stays safe."

They didn't argue. Justin and Jackie crept to the edge of the yard and peered through the leaves into the forest. It was already dark from the thick canopy and was made even darker by the overcast sky.

"I don't hear anything," said Justin.

Jackie put her finger to her lips. "Shhhh." She motioned to him that they should begin walking.

The two began to move, carefully pushing aside branches and slowly easing them back into place so they wouldn't make any extra noise as they entered the woods.

They hadn't taken more than two or three steps when Jackie stopped, staring down toward her feet. "Wow," she said. "Take a look at this."

Chapter Four

Walking on Edge

"Footprints," Justin said. "They're huge!"

"Did you find the moose?" called Nick, who was still not ready to move toward them.

Jackie knelt down. "Those sure are big tracks," she said.

Justin joined her near the ground and asked his next question slowly. "Are they from ... a bear?"

"No way," said Jackie. "They're not shaped right. And there are no claw marks."

"Hey, where are you guys?" called Nick. He couldn't hear them and when they knelt down, he lost sight of them as well.

Jackie quickly scanned more of the soft earth around them. "Hey, there are some different tracks here," she said, and gently rubbed her fingers into a set of smaller impressions.

"It's like two animals were walking together," said Justin. "Maybe it's a dad or mom animal walking with its baby."

"I don't think so," said Jackie, as she began crawling along the ground. "There's a whole trail here. It looks like the big animal was following the smaller animal."

"Do you think it was hunting the poor little animal?" asked Justin.

"That's exactly what I mean," said Jackie.

Justin did not like the look on her face. "What's wrong?" he asked.

"I'm not sure yet what the big animal is," Jackie confessed. "But I think I know what the smaller one is."

Justin nodded, awaiting her reply.

"Dax," she said.

"What?" said Justin. He was stunned. "Do you mean there is some monster animal in our own backyard, waiting to eat my Dax?" This time he didn't wait for her answer. He stood up and burst through the trees and into the yard toward Nick and Dax.

Justin was running so fast, Nick thought he was being chased by something. Leaving Dax behind, he cried out and bolted toward Justin's camp, his binoculars dangling around his neck and beating him in the chest with every frantic stride.

Justin followed closely behind, scooping Dax off the ground as he ran.

Jackie wasn't really afraid, but she still felt butter-flies in her stomach when everyone panicked and took off in such a rush, leaving her all alone. So she ran, too.

In moments, all three stood panting on the front porch of Justin's camp, looking back at the edge of the woods, which seemed a little less threatening from the security of the large, familiar man-made home. The animal wouldn't dare attack them on an enclosed screened-in porch … right? They decided to take turns watching the forest while they talked.

"We've got to make a plan to protect Dax," said Justin. "I can't keep her locked up in our camp for the rest of her life." The cat lingered and slowly wove in and out of their six standing legs. It was like she knew they were talking about her.

"Lock up Dax?" asked Nick. "Why? What was chasing you?"

"Nothing was chasing us," said Jackie. "We just found some tracks that were … unusual."

"They were gigantic," said Justin. "And it looked like whatever was walking out there was hunting Dax."

Nick was distracted. "Hey, haven't you finished your summer puzzle yet?" he asked, and began to sit down at the card table. "Give me ten minutes. I'll bet I can figure out enough of it so you'll know what the picture is supposed to be."

Jackie grabbed Nick by the arm before he could sit and become comfortable. "The only puzzle we are going to work on right now is to find out what that animal out there is," she said. "And I have an idea of what we can do to find out."

Nick was annoyed.

Justin was all ears.

Chapter Five

When You Least Expect It

"Forget Eagle Bay for now," said Jackie. "We're going to Inlet to the hardware store. I think they'll have what we need there."

"Good," said Nick. "I spilled my trail mix all over the yard, running away from the Big Foot. I'll go to the grocery store and get some more."

Justin turned to Jackie. He was irritated. "I don't get it," he said. "I thought you were going to tell us what the big animal is? Why do we need to go to the store?"

Jackie motioned for patience and pulled a small spiral notebook from her back pocket. It was the notebook she was using to write down the names of animals she knew lived around the lake, or to record new animal discoveries. It was slightly bent from all of her sitting and crawling and running around. A short pencil tucked inside the spiral metal spine had somehow managed to survive. She began to recite a short list of supplies, writing each thing down.

"Let's see," Jackie said, thinking out loud. "We'll

need some strips of cardboard, a spoon, a cup and some water." There was a distant low rumble of thunder, and a few large raindrops, the size of nickels, dropped and burst against the porch steps.

"We should have plenty of water," said Nick.

"Come on, Jackie," said Justin. "What is your big idea?"

Jackie continued to write in the notebook. "Okay," she said. "Most of this stuff we already have. You and Nick can go to the grocery store and try to find some vegetable spray, and I'll go to the hardware and get some plaster of paris."

"Paris?" said Nick. "Are we going to Inlet or France?"

There was another rumble of thunder.

"Very funny," Jackie said. "Come on. Let's get to the store before it starts pouring."

"But what do we need vegetable spray and plaster stuff for?" persisted Justin.

"I get it," said Nick. "We're going to cook some food and build a trap to catch the Big Foot – right?"

"Trust me," said Jackie. "You'll see."

Justin grabbed some loose change from the kitchen counter as the three friends headed out the camp's back door. He shoved his small camera deep inside his pocket to keep it from getting wet; and they all took off, dodging raindrops under the ever-darkening clouds.

The short trip down Route 28 to Inlet was made

17

even quicker traveling by bicycle – and safer, thanks to a paved pathway the Town had just completed that ran alongside the busy highway.

Jackie dropped her bike and dashed inside the hardware store while Justin and Nick pedaled a little further and around the corner to the local grocer's.

The two boys bounded up the cement steps and through the front door just as the latest and loudest clap of thunder finally announced the arrival of the official downpour.

The rain erupted from a black-and-purple sky, spraying heavy and in waves as it pounded the thick glass windows and door of the store. It reminded Justin of the way the water looked and sounded from inside the Jeep while moving through a car wash. He felt his pockets – money in one, and his camera dry and secure in the other.

The two young shoppers took their time, carefully examining the items on each shelf, but they could not find the vegetable spray. Actually, they didn't even know what it might look like.

Nick *did* find the ingredients for his special recipe of trail mix. He not only knew what each item looked like, he knew what each one smelled like, tasted like and knew exactly where they were all located. Candy was always up front, near the cash register.

Not one customer was in a hurry to leave and enter the soaking rain. Between flashes of lightning and crashes of thunder, the cashier was busy answering tourists' questions about the local shops and restaurants, so the boys headed back toward the deli and bakery. They thought maybe the person at the counter there would not be so busy and could tell them where they could find the special spray that Jackie insisted they needed.

"This way," said Justin. Moving down the aisle, they passed a large yellow Mosquito Crossing sign that was shaped like a diamond.

"I have the same sign with a giant Black Fly on it in my room," said Nick.

Then it was past the bags of chips and bottled water, finally halting at the bakery and deli.

Nick especially admired the gigantic chocolate chip cookies that sat on silver trays in the large glass case in front of him.

"Can I help you?" asked the worker behind the counter.

"Justin, look," said Nick. "It's a moose."

"Pardon me?" said the clerk.

Justin groped for his camera, and wrestling it from his pocket almost dropped it on the floor. "Where?" he asked, ready to take a picture.

Nick laughed. "Not a real moose," he said, and pointed. "Way up there."

Sure enough, high on the wall above the clerk's head hung a large brown sign in the shape of a moose with the words, **COOKIES: Chocolate Chip – Oatmeal Raisin – Half Moon – 99 cents**.

"How much money did you bring?" Nick asked. "Let's buy one of the dark chocolate chips – they're crunchier." His mouth was watering. "We can split it three ways, easy."

Before Justin could smack his friend for the false moose alarm, there was another rumble of thunder, accompanied by a large crash that came from the cavernous stockroom located right next to them.

"Lightning hit the store!" said Nick. Even the bakery clerk looked concerned.

Together the boys retraced their steps quickly back down the aisle, past the water and chips toward the Mosquito Crossing sign.

They had moved just in time. A white-tailed deer had entered the back of the store and stormed through the open stockroom door. It stood, panting, on the exact spot where they had been only seconds before.

"It must have gotten in where they unload the trucks," said Justin.

Nick looked back over his shoulder at the large, wet animal that somehow looked even larger standing inside the building. "Quick," he said to Justin, "take a picture for Jackie's field guide." Then he rounded the corner and disappeared.

Justin fumbled for his camera again, and nervously lifted it to his eye. That was when the deer, startled by someone yelling from the stockroom, made its next move, galloping down the narrow aisle right at him.

Before Justin could decide what to do, the animal made a sudden awkward turn on its four long, slender legs down another aisle. The animal slid, and then

They had moved just in time. A white-tailed
deer entered the back of the store
and stormed through the open stockroom door.

there was the clatter of hooves against the hardwood floor, followed almost immediately by several screams, as panicked shoppers pressed toward the front door to flee from the store.

This seemed to scare the deer even more, and then there was the sound of cans crashing and rolling all over the floor.

One scream sounded familiar and was very close by. It was Nick, who suddenly reappeared, only to rush by Justin back down the aisle toward the bakery again. "Run!" he said. "It's after me!"

Both boys made a dash for the stockroom. It was the only way out for them, as it was for the frightened doe, which had seen enough flying groceries and shrieking customers to last any wild deer's entire lifetime. The frightened animal was just as anxious as the boys to escape the man-made maze.

"We'll never make it!" said Justin, as the drumming of hooves on the floor behind them grew louder and louder. "Let it run by!"

Nick shifted quickly to stand on one side of the open stockroom door, and Justin leaped on top of some stacked soda cases on the other side.

As the animal galloped toward them, Nick closed his eyes.

Justin teetered on the soda cases and raised the camera.

Click – Click – Click. Three shots, and it was over. The deer charged by them, a brown blur passing from the bakery through the stockroom and out the back door.

"Did you get it? Did you get a picture?" It was Jackie! She didn't care about the rain or wild stampeding deer and had made her way into the store, pushing through the small crowd of fleeing customers, just as the animal was completing its whirlwind tour. As the deer was following the boys, she was following the deer.

Justin jumped down from his cardboard perch and clicked a few buttons on the back of his camera to preview the pictures he had just taken. Jackie and Nick peered over his shoulder as the images quickly appeared.

"Yes!" Justin said. "I got it!" There on the tiny camera screen was a front shot of the doe running through the bakery and deli, flanked on one side by cookies and coleslaw, and dozens of loaves of bread on the other side.

Jackie got out her notebook and pencil and checked off: White-tailed deer – female. "Only 60 more Adirondack mammals left to go," she said. "That is, if all the mammals that live in the Adirondacks live around here."

Justin was surprised. "There are more than sixty different mammals in the Adirondacks?" he said. "I've never heard that before."

"I wonder if that includes the Big Foot we found in the woods," said Nick.

The three Adirondack kids walked through the store that looked like an earthquake had hit it. Cans and boxes and bags were littered everywhere. The

23

store owner excused everyone who was still inside. "We'll reopen in a few hours, folks," he said. "Just give us a little time to clean up."

Distant now were the low rumbles of thunder, and the rain had stopped. A crack in the sky allowed a narrow shaft of sunlight to break through, and the highway suddenly looked as shiny as the side of a silvery minnow.

"A few hours?" said Justin, dismayed. "What about the vegetable spray?" he asked, as they jumped down the cement steps and mounted their bikes for the quick ride back to camp. "How can we do your plan without the vegetable spray?"

"Don't worry," said Jackie. "We can still get started." She held up a small paper bag. "Plaster of paris," she said, and smiled. "Look out, Big Foot, here we come!"

Chapter Six

Making Tracks

The boys were not thrilled with the idea, but Jackie convinced them to return to the edge of the woods. As they moved through the branches, leaves that were heavy with fresh rain droplets brushed against them, soaking their shorts and shirts and skin.

"Where are all the tracks?" said Justin. "There were lots of them an hour ago."

"What are we going to do with all this stuff you made us bring out here?" asked Nick. He was loaded up with supplies Jackie had him carry, including a cup, a plastic spoon, and some long, thin strips of cardboard that were shiny on one side.

Jackie held the small bag of plaster of paris, and Justin, a small bottle of water.

"I was afraid this might happen," Jackie said. "The rain ruined most of the tracks or washed them away." She looked around. "But I can't believe all of them can be gone."

"Let's keep looking," said Justin. "But stay together. The Big Foot shouldn't attack us if we stay close together."

"I found some tracks," said Nick.

Justin and Jackie ran over, looked down at the ground, and sighed.

"No, these tracks look brand new and are totally different," said Jackie. "They are way too small and each one has five toes. The tracks we're looking for are a lot bigger and only have four toes each."

"It's weird," said Justin. "I hardly ever see animals out by the yard, but it looks like they're all over the place."

"Yeah," said Nick. "It's like they just sit in the woods and stare at us all day. It's kind of creepy."

"Animals are always around," said Jackie. "You just have to pay close attention. It's like if you move, the woods sit still. But if you sit still, the woods move."

"Now you're talking really creepy," said Nick. "The next thing you'll be saying is that the branches on these bushes are really long arms that grab you and pick you up." He tugged at a branch with some broad green leaves on it. "Hey, what's this?" he said, glancing at the ground that had been hidden beneath the cover.

"You got one!" said Jackie.

"I did?" said Nick. Suddenly he felt quite important.

"And it's a real good one," said Justin. "It looks like the leaves blocked enough rain and kept it from washing away."

"Wow," said Nick, looking at the track at his feet. "That *is* big."

Jackie dropped to her knees and went right to

work. "Get out the cup and spoon and water," she said. Opening the small container of plaster of paris, she poured some of the powder into the cup. "Put some water in here," she said. "But just a little."

Justin removed the bottle cap and slowly poured water into the cup while Jackie stirred. "How much?" he asked.

"It has to be thick like a milk shake or pancake batter," said Jackie.

Nick suddenly became more interested. "A milk shake? Pancakes?"

"This is track mix – not trail mix!" Jackie said.

Nick frowned.

"I get it," said Justin. "We're going to make sort of a cement copy of the track that's on the ground, right?"

"Yes," said Jackie. She took a thin strip of cardboard from Nick and made a circle around the entire track, pressing the edges firmly into the ground. "I'm putting the shiny part of the cardboard on the inside so the plaster track won't stick to it when we pull it out," she said. Then she poured the mix, completely filling the track and most of the cardboard circle.

"This is actually pretty cool," said Nick. "We should find a whole bunch of different tracks and do this."

"The ground is really wet, so it will take an hour or so for the plaster to dry," Jackie said. She stood up, brushing moist earth off her knees. "We'll come back and get it later. Then we can find a book on animal tracks and see if we can match it, or we'll show it to Ranger Bill. He can probably help us figure out what animal it is."

"All right," said Justin. "I vote we have lunch and come back to pick up the track in exactly one hour."

It was unanimous.

Chapter Seven

Skunked

An hour seemed like a day to Justin, who ate lunch, fed Dax and even took time to change into dry clothes. When he arrived back in the woods, anxious and ahead of schedule, Jackie and Nick were already there.

"It's not quite dry yet," said Jackie, gently pressing her fingers against the surface of the plaster. "It should be ready real soon."

Justin sighed. "Why did it have to rain today?" he said.

Nick was crawling on the ground.

"What are you looking for?" asked Jackie. "We don't need another track."

"I'm looking for a newt," said Nick. "Maybe I'll use some plaster stuff and make some newt tracks."

Jackie couldn't wait. "I'm going to chance it," she said, and slowly tugged the cardboard circle from the grip of the earth. The ease with which it lifted and separated from the ground encouraged her. The cardboard rim dropped away and only the plaster track remained in her hands.

"Wow," said Nick. He reached out to touch it.

Jackie slapped his hand. "Not yet," she said. "You'll break it. Let me wipe it clean. Then we'll take it back to Justin's camp and let it harden really well. Maybe even paint it."

"You're always the boss," said Nick, and walked away unhappy. He looked for Justin, and suddenly realized why his friend was being so quiet – it was because he was missing.

"Over here," whispered Justin. Holding his camera in the shooting position, he was kneeling down and looking out at the yard, using some low branches as cover.

Nick knelt down beside him. "What do you see?" he whispered back. "Is it the Big Foot?"

"A skunk," said Justin. "I think it was sleeping in a log I kicked, and I accidentally woke it up. I got one picture, then it walked out in the yard and over behind the old well. It looks like it found some of the trail mix you spilled."

"I don't see any animal," said Nick, annoyed.

Justin pointed. "See the pump handle?"

Nick nodded.

"The end of the handle is pointing right down at it," Justin said.

"I see it," said Nick. "I think." He shook his head. "But you've got to get a lot closer. You'll never get a good picture from here."

"No way," said Justin. "I don't want to get sprayed."

"You won't get sprayed," said Nick. "Skunks don't spray unless they get really mad or surprised."

Justin shook his head, forcefully. "I am not taking any chances," he said. "My dad said he got sprayed once by a skunk when he was little. He had to take a ton of baths, and he still stunk like a skunk for a week. Besides, some of them can be sick with rabies."

"Look, I think he's moving again," said Nick.

Sure enough, the skunk slowly emerged from the shadow of the old well and was about to resume its leisurely waddle through the yard, when Jackie suddenly burst through the trees toward Justin's camp. Unfortunately, she was also on a direct collision course with the pump, and with the skunk that was hidden from her view.

Justin and Nick tried to warn her. They jumped into the open and yelled her name.

Jackie stopped and smiled at them. "There you are," she said, and held the plaster track out to them. "It came out perfect. You've got to see it." Then she noticed the look on their faces. "What's wrong?" she asked.

They both pointed and shouted at once. "Skunnnnk!"

"Very funny," said Jackie, but the urgency in their voices did cause her to glance down toward her feet. Immediately, she recognized the wide white stripe running down the stocky black back. A pointy black face stared up at her.

"Ruuuunnn!" yelled Justin and Nick.

Jackie felt her legs go weak and she stumbled backward, losing her balance. Before crashing to the ground, she did one-and-a-half cartwheels and then

Jackie felt her legs go weak and she
stumbled backward, losing her balance.

with arms tucked in, rolled across the grass, spinning away from the animal as rapidly as she could.

With a front-row seat to one of the strangest-looking acrobatic acts they had ever seen, Justin and Nick couldn't help it – knowing Jackie was out of danger, they could not stop laughing. The skunk seemed undisturbed and unimpressed and simply strolled away.

The boys ran over to Jackie. "That was the funniest thing I've ever seen," said Nick.

Justin had to agree. "I guess now we know what made those fresh tracks we found in the woods."

Jackie slowly sat up. "Yeah, this is all really funny," she said. Using her fingers as a comb, she began to remove grass and small twigs from her long, blonde hair. "It's just too bad we'll never know what animal made those other tracks."

"What do you mean?" asked Justin. The boys slowly stopped laughing.

Jackie pointed in the direction of the water pump.

There on the cement slab of the well lay the perfect plaster cast of the Big Foot – all smashed in a million tiny pieces.

Chapter Eight

Night Sounds

A million tiny pieces. Justin sat on the camp porch, staring at the bits of puzzle before him on the card table. They kept reminding him of the bits of the shattered plaster cast that had held the key to the identity of the mystery animal lurking just beyond his yard in the woods. *Now we'll never know what that animal was*, he thought, and snapped another puzzle piece into place.

Jackie had felt terrible about the accident and drove her small single-engine boat, the putt-putt, back to her island camp and stayed there for the rest of the day. Justin knew it wasn't her fault the plaster track was broken, and as much as he wanted to, he could not blame her. Nick said he was just glad that for once it was someone else who had an accident, and not him!

The light on the front porch glowed yellow and made the room feel warm, despite the cool breeze that passed through – the air still fresh and clean from the late afternoon rain. A common loon called out over Fourth Lake, a chorus of crickets sang their mid-August tune, and a few flying insects were outside, bouncing against the screens, trying in vain to reach the single, inside bulb.

Justin concentrated, and another puzzle piece found its home on the completed frame. And then another. A pale blue sky with clouds was coming nicely together; and judging from all the other loose pieces stacked on the table in small piles according to their color, it appeared the secret image might be an all-outdoor scene.

Bang!

It had been so peaceful, and he had been so deep in thought, the sudden noise made Justin leap out of his chair.

Bang – Bang!

It sounded like metal. *The garbage can?* he thought. *The Big Foot can't get Dax, so he's hungry for something else!*

He wondered if he should grab for his camera – or a kayak paddle? Or both? He wondered if he should go outside at all?

Bang – Bang —— Bang!

He decided on the camera and a giant flashlight which could double as a weapon, if needed, to protect himself. Since the plaster track was ruined, this might be his only chance to find out the true identity of the Big Foot. His plan was simple. *I'll blind it, take a picture, and run,* he thought. It was the best idea he could come up with on such short notice.

Justin didn't want to disturb his parents. Actually, he thought they might not like the idea of him walking around outside by himself so late at night, especially if they knew he was searching for an unknown animal. They were inside with books, sitting near the fireplace in the main room. Mid-August nights were great for sleeping, and perfect for a small, cozy fire to read by, just before bed.

Still in pajamas, Justin slipped on his hiking boots and crept toward the porch door where he came face to face with some of the oddest-looking creatures on the surface of the planet, which were clinging to the screen. He turned the handle and slowly pushed, trying desperately not to make any noise.

The door squeaked loudly and so he stopped. *It never sounds like this during the day*, he thought. Holding his breath, he tried again. It squeaked again and he stopped again. Using this technique, moving only a fraction of an inch at a time, it seemed to take forever to open the door wide enough to slip outside unnoticed. But patience paid off, and finally he was free and raced across the yard toward the garbage cans.

"Guaranteed animal-proof!" That was his dad's boast to family and neighbors about his latest wood structure encased in chicken wire designed to keep smelly garbage in and hungry creatures out.

Bang Bang – Bang Bang Bang Bang!

Justin flashed his light toward the sound that grew louder as he moved closer. Pointing the wide beam in the direction of the banging, he saw movement inside the cage. The largest can in the center seemed

36

to be rocking back and forth. He moved the light upward. Something was on top of the can.

The Big Foot is here! he thought, and felt small beads of sweat break out on his forehead. But wait. There was more movement, toward the bottom of the can.

It's huge! he thought, and was about to bolt for camp, when he swallowed hard and steadied the light on the action before him.

There on top of the can was one of the largest raccoons he had ever seen. It hesitated only for a moment to peer out at the light, its eyes glowing like an alien from outer space. Then it turned away and went back to work jumping up and down like the lid of the container was a trampoline.

Controlling his panic, he discovered it wasn't one huge animal making all the noise. It was three animals, working as a team, as two more raccoons assisted below at ground level, standing on their hind legs and trying with all their might to help tip the large can over.

Justin's shivers subsided and he headed back to camp, thinking it would be best to confess his late night stroll and tell his parents that the clever masked bandits had found yet another way to break into Dad's latest guaranteed animal-proof invention.

But he did not leave before taking a picture. He held the flashlight by pinching it between his knees and pointed it in the direction of the nighttime thieves. Using his free hands, he lifted the camera to his eye. *Click.*

"Gotcha," he said out loud with satisfaction. *There's still more than 50 animals to go for Jackie's field guide*, he thought, and wondered what animals he and his friends might find tomorrow. *Maybe the missing moose...*

"Justin!" his mom called out into the night.

"Coming!" he called back, and dashed across the yard.

Chapter Nine

Trapped in the Treehouse

Justin was upset. "Why didn't you tell me that Douglas called last night?" he asked his mother. The newest Adirondack kid on the north shore of the lake, Douglas had moved in just three camps up toward Inlet. He was away a lot, and so didn't call often. But when he did call, it was usually important.

"Well, if you were not out in the yard in your pajamas and boots, playing animal detective, you could have taken the call yourself," said Mrs. Robert. She placed a sliced orange on Justin's plate at the breakfast bar.

"But did he say what he wanted?" Justin asked, as he inserted one of the orange slices between his teeth on the left side of his mouth. He bit down hard and the slice burst like a fruit bomb – the juice filling his mouth and streaming cool and sweet down his throat.

Mrs. Robert dried her hands with a paper towel. "He said he wouldn't be home today, but wanted you and your friends to know that there was an animal in his yard you would probably want to know about."

"What?" said Justin. "How could you not tell me? Maybe it's the moose." He stuffed the remaining orange slices into his mouth, grabbed his camera and orange bucket hat and headed out the door.

His mother smiled and, holding the door ajar, called after him. "He said you can only see it from the treehouse."

Tired of being cooped up inside the camp for hours, Dax had been waiting to escape, and Justin's mom had just provided the perfect opportunity.

"Oh, dear," said Mrs. Robert, as the clever cat darted by her legs and out the door.

Justin ran all the way through Pioneer Village and reaching Nick's camp out of breath, pounded on the back door. It was early and no one answered. He listened. There was no sound.

He paced back and forth for only a moment and decided not to wait. Bolting for the narrow path that followed the edge of the lake leading to Douglas's camp, he didn't stop running until he had reached one of the three massive treehouses that overlooked entire sections of his friend's property.

Which treehouse? he wondered, and thought maybe he should have asked his mom more questions before leaving in such a hurry. *What if Douglas had left more information?* He scanned the ground for footprints and the tree limbs above for any movement. Not seeing or hearing anything, he ran to the second treehouse. Nothing unusual there either.

40

I hope Douglas wasn't kidding, Justin thought, as he headed for the third and last treehouse. That was when his mother's words came back to him – 'You can only see it *from* the treehouse.'

There was a noise behind him and his heart leaped. It was Nick.

"You scared me," said Justin, but he was really glad to have his friend at his side again.

"You took off before I could even answer the door," Nick said. "I saw you head for the path, but I had to finish making my trail mix." He held up his bag and grinned. Then he looked around. "So, where's Douglas? What are we doing here, anyway?"

Before Justin could explain, they were interrupted by another noise. A deep grunt. They turned to find a black bear was slowly making its way in their direction.

"Quick! Climb!" said Justin.

Nick didn't need to be told. He was already half-way up the wooden ladder of the treehouse, with Justin's hands closely behind his scrambling sneakers. Once inside, they both reached down and pulled on the ladder which scoped upward and out of the bear's reach.

Or so they thought …

A black bear was slowly making its
way in their direction. Justin and Nick
hurried into the treehouse.

Chapter Ten

A Prickly Situation

The bear came to a stop below the treehouse where a large bird feeder was attached to a short pole. The feeder was empty. And so was the bear's stomach, which was driving the animal to make its rounds to some familiar dining spots.

As the bear paced the ground below, the two boys paced the treehouse floor above.

It was a house all right. A house in the trees. They had not known Douglas very long, and neither of the boys had ever actually been inside one of the impressive structures before.

"This would make a great clubhouse," said Nick.

Justin nodded and guessed it was half the size of the sleeping porch. There were benches against the inside walls all the way around and even two small Adirondack chairs in two corners. Electricity fed lights both inside and out, and while screens on the large windows kept out most bugs, the tree that grew up the center of the house was home to its own families of creeping and crawling residents. "Jackie wouldn't like the spiders," he said.

"I sure hope Dax stays safe," said Nick, still peering down at the bear, whose snout was buried in the ground in search of seed at the foot of the bird feeder.

"Of course Dax is safe," said Justin, as he snapped a picture of the hungry animal. "I left her back at camp and I'm not letting her out until we find the Big Foot."

"That's funny," said Nick.

"What?" asked Justin.

Nick hesitated. "Well, when I watched you run down the path, I saw Dax running right behind you."

"No way," said Justin. That's all he could say, and just kept repeating the phrase as he moved from window to window for any sign of her. "No way. No way."

While the two trapped boys scoured the grounds for some sign of Dax, Nick noticed a strange bump on a slim tree trunk just several feet from one of the treehouse windows. "Hey, look at this," he said.

"Did you find Dax?" asked Justin, hopefully.

Nick pointed out at the slender tree trunk.

"It's a porcupine," said Justin. The mammal, with long dark fur that mingled with grayish quills, clung to the tree, motionless. "That must be the animal Douglas called me about."

"So *that's* why you came over here," said Nick.

"Yes," said Justin. "But I really don't care about some dumb old porcupine and field guide right now."

The bear grunted again and continued to walk back and forth below the treehouse.

"Why won't it just go away?" said Justin.

44

Nick pulled out his bag of trail mix. "Well, at least if we get stuck up here, we'll have plenty to eat," he said, and offered a handful to his friend.

"Not now," said Justin, annoyed. "I've already had breakfast." He pushed Nick's hand away sending the trail mix into flight. They both watched helplessly as the colored rain slowly descended through the air and peppered the head of the hungry bear below.

The bear appreciated the free candy shower, and immediately devoured the small puddle of sweets.

"I don't like this," said Nick. "I don't like this at all."

"Why did you feed the bear?" asked Justin.

Nick defended himself. "It's your fault," he argued. "You knocked the trail mix out of my hand."

They heard a loud crack and the treehouse shook.

Looking back down they saw the bear, now standing on its hind legs, had reached the bottom rung and pulled the entire ladder back down to the ground. The rung had snapped under the bear's immense weight, causing the entire tree to shake. The boys knew it was hopeless to try and wrestle the ladder back up. They tried yelling, but the bear was on a mission. He liked Nick's breakfast food and wanted more.

"What are we going to do?" asked Nick.

Justin had no answer.

A muffled voice sounded from somewhere behind them.

"Hello, Nick? Justin? Can you hear me? Over."

"Hey, it sounds like Jackie," said Nick. He could not believe how glad he was to hear her.

"But where is she?" asked Justin.

The familiar voice sounded again. "Justin? Nick? Are you out there? Over."

As the bear wrestled with the ladder, the boys frantically searched the treehouse for the source of Jackie's voice. They even looked outside the windows, wondering if, like the porcupine, she had somehow managed to climb up a tree next to them.

"Look!" said Nick. "A walkie-talkie! This place has everything!"

It was true. There on the back of the tree trunk in the center of the house hung the welcomed communication device.

Justin grabbed it from the nail that held it, pushed a red button and answered. "Jackie, where are you? We need help! Over."

"I'm in the treehouse next to the lake," she said. "What's wrong? Where are you? Over."

Nick grabbed the walkie-talkie from Justin's hand. "We're over in the treehouse near the parking lot – by the bird feeder," he said. "A bear is trying to eat us. Hurry over! Before it's all over! Over!"

The treehouse shook again. The boys watched in horror, as the bear looked like it was actually trying to climb the ladder. It snapped a second rung.

The reply they had hoped for came through the crackling and static. "We're on our way," said Jackie. "Over."

"Did you hear her?" said Nick. "She's not alone! How long do you think it will take them to get here?"

"I don't know, but I have an idea," said Justin. He walked to the treehouse door, leaned out and pointed his camera toward the bear that was peering up at them.

Nick shook his head. "We are going to get eaten and you want to take a picture?"

Justin pushed a button and the camera's flash went off. The timing was perfect. Just as the light from the flash seemed to temporarily blind the bear, Jackie arrived with an old hubcap and a crowbar she had taken from Douglas's garage. She began yelling and banging them together with all her might.

Was it the camera flash from above, or the clanging metal from behind, or both? The three Adirondack kids could not tell for sure, but the bear seemed confused and finally ran away and out of sight.

"Dax!" said Justin, and then he realized who was with Jackie when she called on the walkie-talkie.

Nick snatched the camera to take a picture of the porcupine as Justin hurried down the ladder to be reunited with his calico beauty. He picked her up in his arms and scolded her. "What are you doing outside?" he said. "I'm taking you back to camp right now where it's safe."

"Come on down, Nick," called Jackie. "We don't have time to hang around here."

Justin looked around. "Is the bear coming back?"

"It's not that," said Jackie, as Nick trotted over to join them. "I called the newspaper again this morning about the moose."

"Oh, no," said Justin. "Did somebody already get a picture?"

Jackie shook her head. "No," she said. "The moose was seen last night at dusk – headed straight for Eagle Bay."

Chapter Eleven

Rocky Mountain Spies

Justin was happy with Jackie's latest idea. Not only because he thought it would give them an advantage in spotting the moose, but because in all of his more than ten years of life, as close to his camp as it was, he had never once climbed Rocky Mountain.

Of course, Jackie climbed the small mountain all the time. It was one of her favorite places to go – to be alone – to think – and to just look down at her island camp on Fourth Lake. But you could also see for miles, including bird's-eye views of Eagle Bay and Inlet.

Dropping their bikes in the parking lot along Route 28 near the trailhead, the three Adirondack kids passed quickly between the large boulder and fallen log to sign in at the register. Then they began the short march, following the yellow trail markers, using roots and rocks as steps to rise toward the sky. It was only a half-mile from the trailhead to the summit along the easy path. In fact, Jackie usually ran up the mountain – but not with Nick along.

"Can we slow down a little?" asked Nick.

"No," said Jackie.

Nick complained. "Why not?" he asked. "We haven't stopped one time since we started climbing."

Jackie timed her answer perfectly. "Because we're already here," she said, as they suddenly walked out onto the wide, open rock face that was the mountain summit.

"Whoa," said Nick, who caught a glimpse of Fourth Lake, and charged ahead for a better view.

Jackie called after him. "I thought you were tired?"

Justin was equally excited, but he didn't run. He actually slowed down for a moment, almost as if walking in a trance, and stared out at the lake that had been his home for ten summers. The water seemed to stretch out on the horizon as far as he could see.

They caught up to Nick, who was already standing along the edge of a rock shelf, facing westward toward Eagle Bay. "I don't see the moose yet," he said.

Justin reached over and used the palm of his hand to cover Nick's mouth. "Shhhh," he said, and turned to see if any of the other early morning climbers on the summit had heard his friend's comment. "We don't want to give anyone else our idea."

"That's strange," said Jackie. "There aren't many boats on the lake, but what few there are, are all bunched together in the bay near the north shore." She turned to Nick. "Give me the binoculars. Quick."

The boys followed her further along the rock face where there was a fuller view of Route 28 where it passed through Eagle Bay. Jackie lifted the binoculars

Nick was already standing along the edge
of a rock shelf, looking westward toward Eagle Bay.
"I don't see the moose yet," he said.

and focused on the center of the small hamlet below.

"What do you see?" asked Nick.

Justin used to be really annoyed with his friend, who always seemed to butt in and ask questions first. But as time went by, it bothered him less and less, because he always seemed to ask the very same questions he would ask anyway.

"There are a lot of cars backed up on the highway," said Jackie. "Right in front of the cafe." She pulled the field glasses away from her face and groaned with frustration. "How do you adjust these things?"

"Let me try," said Justin. He grabbed the glasses and worked on focusing the lenses for a clearer view of the distant scene. "Yes," he said. "Everybody is stopped and it looks like a horse is standing right in the middle of the highway."

Nick shrugged. "Big deal," he said. "Probably one of the horses got loose from the stable down the Uncas Road."

"Wait a minute," said Justin. "Horses don't have antlers."

"No," said Jackie. "But a deer does."

"A unicorn has a horn," offered Nick. "Maybe it's a unicorn."

Jackie looked at him. "You're not serious," she said, and laughed. Nick just stared back at her, and she stopped laughing. "Are you?" she asked.

Justin interrupted. "It's not a horse," he said, still straining for visual clues. "It's not a deer, either. And it's sure not a unicorn."

Someone near them with a long telescope set up on a tripod made the announcement the Adirondack kids had been waiting for two long days to hear.

"It's a moose," the stranger said to anyone who would listen. "Anybody want to take a look? There's definitely a moose down on the highway in Eagle Bay."

As people lined up to take a turn looking through the friendly hiker's telescope, there were three young climbers who were already out of sight, headed back down the mountain.

Chapter Twelve

Mapping Out a Plan

By the time the Adirondack kids had reached their bikes and pedaled to Eagle Bay so fast that it felt like their leg muscles were on fire, the excitement was already over. Jackie ran into the grocery store to see if she could get some information from anyone inside.

"No traffic jam. No moose. No picture," said Nick, who was panting, thirsty and hungry.

Justin shook his head. "Somebody must have taken a picture by now," he said. "If we don't find the moose today, I know it will be too late."

Jackie returned with excitement in her voice. "Okay, a lady in the check-out line told me that the moose headed off into the woods, and that a lot of people drove down Big Moose Road hoping to see it again."

"Big Moose Road?" said Nick. "That's probably where it lives. Let's find it."

"Well, we can't just go – we've got to get permission," said Justin.

Jackie offered another plan. "Let's go back to camp and get some water and a map," she said.

"Then we can ask permission, and by looking at the map, maybe figure out where the moose might go." Justin hesitated. Like Nick, he really wanted to follow the crowd down Big Moose Road and get that photograph now, but he knew checking in at camp was the right thing to do. "All right," he said. "But we have to hurry."

"Chores?" Justin said, when he asked for permission to bike down Big Moose Road. He couldn't believe it. "But, Mom … "

Nick was home having lunch, and Jackie was off to her island home to find a map. Justin's job was to clean up the mess the raccoons had made the night before. Then he would be free to explore with his friends.

The day was melting away quickly, as late morning became early afternoon. With chores completed and lunch consumed, Justin and Nick waited on the dock for Jackie's return. Her single engine putt-putt was cutting across the lake at a good rate of speed. It didn't take long before the silver vessel was thumping against the bumper pads of the dock.

"I've got the map," she said, as they helped her tie up the boat.

"Great," said Justin. "Let's go."

"Wait," said Jackie. "We have a decision to make." She knelt and spread out the map on the dock in front of her. "Help me hold it down," she said, as a slight breeze threatened to lift the thin paper up and away like a wild kite without a string.

They each took a corner, pinning the map to the dock boards with their knees. Dax joined them and sat on the fourth corner.

"You let Dax outside?" said Nick, amazed.

Justin sighed. "Mom told me I had to," he said. "But just for a little while."

Jackie pointed to a spot on the map. "The lady at the store said the moose went into the woods about here," she said. "So, these are our choices. We can either bike up Big Moose Road and look for it, or we can ride up the Uncas Road. The moose has to be somewhere between the two roads."

"I vote we go up Big Moose Road," said Nick. "It's got the word moose in it."

"And all the cars went that way," said Justin. But he knew Jackie had to have a reason for even suggesting another way. "Why go up the Uncas Road at all?"

Jackie ran her finger along a faint, squiggly green line on the map. "This is Eagle Creek," she said. "I think the moose might stop and turn and walk along the creek." Then she ran her finger along a squiggly black line right next to the faint green one. "And the creek runs close by the Uncas Road." She sat up straight with her knees still on the map and her hands on her hips. "So, let's vote. I say, Uncas Road."

Justin shook his head. "Me, too," he said. "I vote Uncas Road."

Nick was outnumbered, but Jackie and Justin hoped he would agree with them.

"I don't know," Nick said.

Jackie gathered the map to fold it up. "That's a maybe," she said. "And a maybe is yes!"

Chapter Thirteen

Follow the Salmon Brick Road

"I don't know if this was such a great idea," said Justin, as the three friends biked side by side down the lonely Uncas Road. "There's nothing here at all."

"I told you so," said Nick. "We should have gone down Big Moose, like everybody else."

Jackie refused to be discouraged. "You brought your camera, right, Justin?"

He nodded.

She turned to Nick as they pedaled onward, their tires bumping on small rocks and pebbles that were littered all along the narrow, dusty dirt road. He was wearing a small daypack. "And you brought the binoculars, right, Nick?"

"Yes, I brought the binoculars," he said. "And I brought some other great stuff, too."

"I'll bet," said Jackie. "Like a pound of trail mix."

Nick frowned at her.

Justin was busy trying to imagine what it would be like to take a picture of the moose. How close might they get? Would they see the moose at all?

A horn honked behind them, and they swerved to

form a single file and let the car go by.

"One car, that's all we've seen," said Nick. "I vote we go back right now."

Jackie kicked back suddenly on her brakes, and the two boys skidded to a stop beside her.

"Finally," said Nick. "I wonder what's for supper tonight?"

"You don't agree with him, do you?" said Justin. He pleaded with her. "We can't stop now. I know this is our last chance."

Jackie smiled. "We're not going back," she said, and pointed to a brown sign with yellow letters that marked a small parking area nearly hidden from view on the side of the road.

Nick began slowly reading the sign out loud. "Pigeon Lake Wilderness Area," he said, and groaned. "Now we're looking for pigeons? I'm not walking through the woods looking for a bunch of pigeons."

Justin kept reading. "Ferd's Bog Trail … " His eyes widened. "I know about this place," he said. "My dad comes here all the time to take pictures of birds."

Nick shook his head. "You said you wanted to find the moose – not birds." He pointed to the sign. "Look. It's 30 miles away. We'll never be home in time for supper – probably not even in time for breakfast tomorrow."

"That's not 30 miles," said Jackie. "See the little dot in front of the 3? That's .30 miles. It's about the same as walking around the track at school one time. That's way less than even one mile." She walked her bike into the parking area, flipped the kickstand, and jogged up to the trail register. "I'm signing us in."

Justin leaned his bike against a tree and joined her.

"This isn't fair," said Nick, as he dropped his bike to the ground. "We don't even vote any more."

The soft earth of the friendly winding trail leading toward the bog seemed to absorb any sound made by their sneakers and boots, allowing them to move through the woods silently. Only once did they even have to bend over to scramble underneath an old tree trunk that had fallen and blocked the path.

"I don't hear any pigeons," said Nick. "I don't hear any chirping at all."

"That's because it's so late in the summer," Jackie said. "Besides, we aren't looking for birds, remember?"

While Nick and Jackie continued to argue, Justin was looking back and forth into the woods for any sign of the moose. It was so still and so quiet. He began to think their mission was hopeless.

Nick stubbed his boot and went tumbling to the ground. "Who put a sidewalk in the middle of the woods?" he said, as Justin and Jackie helped him to his feet.

"It's not a sidewalk," Justin said. "It's a boardwalk."

"So what's it doing way out here?" asked Nick. "Does somebody live in the bog?"

"It's to keep us from sinking," said Justin.

Now he had both Nick's and Jackie's full attention.

"That's what my dad told me," said Justin. "Bogs

are wet and squishy, so they put in a boardwalk to keep people from stepping all over and ruining everything."

"But you said it was to keep people from sinking," said Nick. "What does *that* mean?"

Justin sighed. "It means that if you step in the wrong place in a bog, you can sink way in. One time, my dad saw a guy sink in all the way up to his waist."

"Do you mean like in quicksand?" Nick said. "I'm too short. I'd sink in up to my neck. I'm not going out there."

Jackie shrugged. "It's not scary to me," she said. "We'll just stay on the boardwalk. That's what it's here for." She stepped up and tapped it with her boot. "It kind of reminds me of the Yellow Brick Road, except this is more of a tan or salmon color."

"Everything reminds you of that *Wizard of Oz* movie," said Nick. "Did you forget about the poison flowers and flying monkeys in the woods? What about them?" He looked up into the trees for any sign of trouble on wings. "Just thinking about it gives me the creeps."

"Let's go," said Justin, and jumped up to join Jackie. "Let's follow the Salmon Brick Road."

"I'll do it," said Nick, as he adjusted the small pack on his back and stepped forward. "But Jackie has to promise not to start singing."

The woods thinned out as, side by side, the Adirondack kids marched forward.

The boardwalk slightly moved under their combined weight as its lazy curves led them further out into the open. Nick didn't like the floating feeling at all. "We're sinking," he said, but was distracted by a shape darting through the air. "Hey, was that a pigeon?"

"Cedar waxwing," said Jackie. "That's one of the few birds we're likely to see out here this time of year."

Rounding the boardwalk's final curve, they walked the last few hundred feet of runway that led straight out to a large platform.

"That's it," said Justin." The three Adirondack kids stood surrounded by what appeared to be a wide open field bordered by evergreen trees. The long brown and green grass of the bog was the only thing moving in the easy breeze.

Jackie pointed. "There's the creek," she said. "It's not very wide."

Nick dropped his pack on the decking, pulled out his binoculars, and slowly began to scan the area.

"Nothing, right?" said Justin.

"Not a creature is stirring – not even a moose," said Nick. He waited for some laughter. "Get it? Not even a *moose*."

"Yes, we got it," said Jackie. "Not funny."

Nick turned to face them. "It's not my fault there's nothing here," he said. "I told you we should have taken – big moose … " His voice trailed off.

"I know," said Justin. "Why do you keep rubbing it in?"

"Big moose!" said Nick.

"Stop it, Nick," warned Jackie. "Justin already feels bad enough."

"No. No. No." Nick pointed. "It's a moose, a big moose!"

Justin and Jackie slowly turned. Nick was wrong. It wasn't a big moose. It was a gigantic moose.

"Where did it come from?" Nick said, his voice shaking. "It must have been walking right behind us."

"I don't think it's seen us yet," said Justin, hopefully. The animal turned its head and looked straight at them.

"It has now," said Jackie.

All 1400 pounds of muscle, fur and antlers continued walking down the boardwalk, slowly bearing down on them.

"It's blocking our only way out of here," cried Nick. "You read the story in the paper. It ripped the stuffed bear in Old Forge to pieces. What will it do to us?" The moose moved closer. Nick cried out. "We're doomed!"

All 1400 pounds of muscle, fur and
antlers began walking down the boardwalk,
slowly bearing down on them.

Chapter Fourteen

Mission Accomplished – Almost

"We've got to get into the bog," said Justin.

"No way!" said Nick. "We'll sink in and disappear!"

"We don't have a choice, Nick," said Jackie. "We've just got to be careful where we put our feet."

Nick held his breath as the three friends all held hands and gently stepped off the solid boardwalk and out into the bog together. They continued to face the moose to keep an eye on it. The moist mat of grasses and roots under their feet felt more firm than they all had imagined it would be.

"It bounced a little, but it's okay," said Nick, relieved.

They took two steps backward. Justin felt a slight tear in the ground and could suddenly feel water seeping through his sneakers and socks. He hoped Nick's boots were waterproof so he wouldn't panic more.

They weren't, and he did.

"Oh, no," said Nick. "My feet are sinking in! Wait. Okay, it stopped."

The moose paused.

"Take a picture," said Jackie.

"Are you kidding?" said Justin.

Jackie reached toward Justin's pocket. "Then give the camera to me," she said.

"All right, I'll do it," said Justin, as he fumbled for his camera.

The moose looked back over its shoulder.

Nick peered through his binoculars to see what the moose might be looking at. "We're saved," he said. "It's two people."

Justin lifted the camera to take a picture.

"Oh no," said Nick.

Justin lowered the camera. "What's wrong?"

"It looks like those people have a camera, too," Nick said.

Now it was the moose that was trapped. It looked back at the three kids standing low in the bog. Then it turned to step off the boardwalk and toward the cover of the nearby forest.

"Hurry, Justin, take the picture," Jackie said.

Justin lifted the camera and pressed the button to take the shot.

Nothing happened.

"What's wrong?" asked Jackie.

"The moose is leaving," said Nick.

"The camera card is full," said Justin. Frantically, he began to push some buttons. "I need time to take some pictures off the camera card so I can make room for new ones."

"Don't erase the deer in the grocery store," said Jackie. "Or the bear by the treehouse."

"Don't get rid of Jackie and the skunk," said Nick.

"I'll get rid of Dax," said Justin. "I can get a picture of her anytime."

"Don't bother," said Jackie.

"Why not?" said Justin, frustrated that he knew so little about his new camera.

"Because the moose is gone," Jackie said.

"And so are the people with the camera," said Nick. He rested the binoculars on his chest.

Justin lowered the camera and slowly slipped it back into his pocket. The look of disappointment on his face said far more about his feelings than any words that he might say.

"Hey, can we get out of here, now?" said Nick. He lifted one of his soaking feet. It stuck for a moment and then pulled free, making a sucking sound. "My toes feel like prunes."

Chapter Fifteen

Puzzled

It had been several long rainy days since the close encounter with the moose in Ferd's Bog. Justin finally decided it was time to download onto the camp computer the many photographs of other animals he had taken over the past weekend.

While the camera and computer were talking to each other, Justin was talking to himself. A copy of the *Weekly Adirondack* newspaper was next to him where he sat working at the card table on the few remaining pieces of the camp puzzle. Someone had finally taken a picture of the mystery moose that had kept appearing and disappearing all along the Fulton Chain of Lakes. It just wasn't *his* picture.

There on the front page of the paper were several images of the huge animal. A few of the photos had been taken by people who had seen the moose in Eagle Bay. But the biggest picture, front and center and above the fold, was a full head shot of the moose where it stood on the boardwalk in Ferd's Bog. There was a smaller picture next to it of the person who took the winning picture. She was holding a check for $100.

Justin snapped a puzzle piece into place and it snapped his mind to full attention back on the challenge in front of him. The puzzle was obviously an outdoor scene of a forest with an animal standing on some large rocks. The question in recent days had been – what animal? The piece he had just put into place revealed a long furry tip of an odd-looking ear. He spread out the remaining stack of pieces that were all the same color.

Another piece of the puzzle found its proper home and then a small group of five pieces that were the animal's piercing eyes suddenly made sense and fit in together all at once. Justin loved it when he was working on a puzzle and that happened.

It looks like a cat of some kind, he thought. *But what kind of cat?*

The front door swung open and Nick and Jackie barged in to get out of the rain.

"Aren't you done with that puzzle yet?" asked Nick, who reached out to help.

Justin pushed him away. "Don't touch anything with your soaking wet hands," he said.

"Okay," said Nick. He grabbed the back of Justin's shirt and dried off as fast as he could before his friend could pull away. "There," he said, holding up his hands for Justin's approval. "All dry."

Justin was now too involved in the puzzle to fight, and the three friends hovered over the card table and worked together to sort and match pieces in an effort to expose the animal's true identity.

"I almost have the face done," Justin said, as he connected two more pieces.

"It sure looks mean," said Nick, adding another.

Jackie was busy off to the side, working on a large portion of the animal's body. She picked up an entire section she had successfully linked together. Twenty-four fingers and six thumbs helped ease and press it into place.

"It is definitely a cat," said Justin.

"Not like any cat I've ever seen before," said Nick.

"I think I know what it is," said Jackie.

Before she could answer, Justin's mom called from inside the cabin. "Those photos must be loaded by now, Justin," she said. "Please check, because I have some work I need to do on the computer."

"Let's see them," said Jackie.

Justin was still upset there was no picture of a moose, but her enthusiasm lifted his spirit.

Huddled around the computer screen in the cabin's library, the Adirondack kids studied the animal pictures one by one: The deer. The skunk. The bear. The porcupine.

"You're a pretty good picture-taker," Nick said. He especially liked the look on Jackie's face in the picture where she nearly stepped on the skunk.

Last to pop up on the computer screen were the pictures of Dax. Justin started clicking through them quickly.

"Wait a minute," said Jackie. "You're going too fast. Go back."

Justin sighed, and began clicking the pictures backwards. "You didn't even want me to take any pictures of Dax. Remember? Now you want to see them in slow motion?"

"Stop there," said Jackie.

"Big deal," said Nick. "It's Dax sitting on the ground. Justin has a million pictures of her like that already."

"No," said Jackie. She pointed. "Look in the woods behind her. See it?"

Justin's eyes widened. "Yes," he said. He punched a few buttons on the computer to enlarge the background of the picture.

"Wow," said Nick. "It's the same animal that's in the puzzle!"

Chapter Sixteen

The Missing Lynx

Mr. Robert hung up the phone. He looked grim.
Justin, Jackie and Nick were trying to be patient.
Seeing the look on Mr. Robert's face was not encouraging.

"What did the newspaper people say, Dad?" asked Justin.

Mr. Robert began slowly. "Well … " he said. His sober look turned suddenly into a broad smile. "Well, they said you may have taken the Adirondack Photo of the Year."

The Adirondack kids cheered.

"You scared me, Dad," said Justin.

"Several people have claimed to have seen a lynx in recent years, but no one has had hard proof that the animal is still here in the Adirondacks – until you took your pictures," said Mr. Robert. "The people at the *Weekly Adirondack* don't normally pay for pictures, but yours will be on the front page next week. It would not surprise me at all if you get more calls from other newspapers and magazines."

"Just think," said Nick. "You almost erased the

pictures of Dax to make room for the missing moose. Instead you found the missing lynx."

"Wait – there's more," said Mr. Robert. "They also want to print the collection of photographs you took of all the other animals to show how people and wild animals live side by side in the Adirondacks. The deer in the store. The bear at the feeder. The raccoons on the cans. The skunk at the well. It's quite a series. I wish I'd thought of the idea myself." He turned to Jackie. "But they will only print the pictures if you agree to write descriptions of each animal – like in a field guide."

Jackie beamed. "They want me to write for a real newspaper?" she said. "Of course I'll do it."

"What do they want me to do?" asked Nick.

"Give them your trail mix recipe," said Jackie.

Nick scowled at her.

"You took the picture of the porcupine, remember?" said Justin.

Nick stood a little taller. "Oh, yeah, I almost forgot," he said, and grinned.

Mrs. Robert entered the room with Dax. "Just to let you know, I am letting her outside now," she said.

Everyone followed as she headed for the front porch.

"But, Mom," said Justin. "There is a lynx out there."

"Which is long gone by now," said Mr. Robert. "It is possible no one will ever catch a glimpse of that animal anywhere ever again."

Justin looked doubtful.

The jailed cat sensed where Mrs. Robert was

73

heading and lunged from her arms toward freedom. Before landing, she slid across the card table, sending the completed camp puzzle flying through the air. The screen door opened, and she disappeared. The lynx disintegrated upon impact with the floor.

"Don't worry," said Mr. Robert. "Dax will be safe. I promise."

The jailed cat lunged from
the card table toward freedom.

epilogue

"I made you famous," Justin said to Dax. He was taping the front page of the *Weekly Adirondack* onto the ceiling of the sleeping porch. The large picture of Dax with the lynx would hang right above his bed where he could look at it every night.

Jackie had collected a bunch of copies of the paper that contained her first field guide to send to her relatives all across the country, and was even planning to send a copy to an aunt who lived across the ocean in Ireland.

And Nick? He was somewhere out in the woods with plaster and cardboard and water, looking for more animal tracks.

Justin finished securing the page to the ceiling with more tape and then dropped back down onto the bed. Dax jumped up from the floor to join him. *Dad was right*, he thought, as he buried his fingers into the fur of her neck. Another week had gone by, and there was no sign of the lynx or the moose or any other unusual or dangerous animals. Dax was safe.

He laid back and folded his hands behind his head on the pillow.

He was bored again, but there was no way he was going to tell his mother.

 **DAX FACTS**

MAKING TRACKS

Making plaster casts of animal tracks is fun and easy with the right materials. Just be sure to have permission from an adult!

Needed are:
- ❑ Plaster of paris
- ❑ Water
- ❑ Spoon and paper cup (*for mixing*)
- ❑ Strips of flexible cardboard (*one – two feet long and two – four inches wide*).
- ❑ A clean animal track!

Make Tracks by:
- ❑ Mixing plaster of paris with water until it is creamy like pancake batter.
- ❑ Form a ring around the animal track with your cardboard strip.
- ❑ Pour the mixture into the animal track and let it dry (*wet tracks take longer to dry*).
- ❑ When the plaster is completely dry, lift your track straight up. An animal track field guide can help you identify the animal you have found!

The Moose

The **moose** is the largest member of its family – the deer family. Some stand over 6 feet tall and weigh more than 1000 pounds! They range in color from dark brown to a light beige.

Only male moose have antlers, and just one set can weigh up to 90 pounds. These are shed every year before winter.

There are over two hundred moose in the Adirondacks today; and they are doing so well, some experts think within the next ten years there could be over five hundred in the Park!

Several moose hot spots in the Adirondacks include the Moose River Plains, Perkins Clearing region,

Moose. *Photograph ©2007 Eric Dresser*

Honnedaga Lake in the West Canada Creek area in Herkimer and Hamilton Counties, and Mecham Lake in Franklin County.

Because of the size of these mammals, they can create quite a stir wherever they may show up – like stopping traffic and hanging around with cows at farms.

Seeing a moose in the six-million-acre Adirondack Park is rare. If you see one, consider yourself lucky!

The Lynx

Many years ago the **lynx** completely disappeared from the Adirondacks. There have been attempts to release lynx in the Adirondack Park to help them return to the region, but with very little success. Every now and then, someone claims to have seen one of the animals, which is the size of a larger cat, and is sometimes confused with its cousin, the bobcat.

A lynx has a flared facial ruff and tufts of fur, which are usually black, on its ears. The tail is usually short and its wide feet act as snowshoes. The main meal for a lynx is the snowshoe hare.

Most wild lynx live to about fifteen years of age, but some which are kept in captivity have lived as long as twenty-one years.

Lynx. *Photograph ©2007 Eric Dresser*

 **DAX FACTS**

Mammals of the Adirondacks

There are over sixty known mammals in the Adirondacks. What follows is a list arranged in alphabetical order of those you might find. A good field guide can help you identify them. How many have you seen?

❑ Beaver
  (Castor canadensis)

❑ Big Brown Bat
  (Eptesicus fuscus)

Black Bear (Old Split Ear).
Photograph ©2007 Gary VanRiper

❑ Black Bear
  (Ursa americana)

❑ Bobcat *(Lynx rufus)*

❑ Canada Lynx
  (Lynx canadensis)

❑ Coyote *(Canis latrans)*

❑ Deer Mouse
  (Peromyscus maniculatus)

❑ Eastern Chipmunk
  (Tamias striatus)

❑ Eastern Cottontail
  (Sylvilagus floridanus)

❑ Eastern Pipistrelle
  (Pipistrellus subflavus)

❑ Ermine
  (Mustela erminea)

❑ European Hare
  (Lepus europaeus)

❑ Fisher *(Martes pennanti)*

❑ Gray Fox
  (Urocyon cinereoargenteus)

- ❏ Gray Squirrel
  (Sciurus carolinensis)
- ❏ Hairy-tailed Mole
  (Parascalops breweri)
- ❏ Hoary Bat
  (Lasiurus cinereus)
- ❏ House Mouse
  (Mus musculus)
- ❏ Indiana Bat
  (Myotis sodalis)
- ❏ Keen's Myotis
  (Myotis keeni)
- ❏ Little Brown Bat
  (Myotis lucifigus)
- ❏ Long-tailed Shrew
  (Sorex dispar)
- ❏ Long-tailed Weasel
  (Mustela frenata)
- ❏ Man *(Homo sapiens)*
- ❏ Marten
  (Martes americana)
- ❏ Masked Shrew
  (Sorex cinereus)
- ❏ Meadow Jumping
  Mouse *(Zapus hudsonius)*
- ❏ Meadow Vole
  (Microtus pennsylvanicus)
- ❏ Mink *(Mustela vison)*
- ❏ Moose *(Alces alces)*

- ❏ Muskrat
  (Ondatra zibethicus)
- ❏ New England
  Cottontail
  (Sylvilagus transitionalis)
- ❏ Northern Bog
  Lemming
  (Synaptomys borealis)
- ❏ Northern Flying
  Squirrel
  (Glaucomys sabrinus)
- ❏ Norway Rat
  (Rattus norvegicus)
- ❏ Opossum
  (Didelphis virginiana)

Porcupine.
Photograph ©2007 Gary VanRiper

- ❏ Porcupine
  (Erithizon dorsatum)

❑ Pygmy Shrew
(Sorex hoyi)

Raccoon.
Photograph ©2007 Eric Dresser

❑ Raccoon *(Procyon lotor)*

❑ Red-Backed Vole
(Clethrionomys papperi)

❑ Red Bat
(Lasiurus borealis)

❑ Red Fox
(Vulpes vulpes)

❑ Red Squirrel
(Tamiasciurus hudsonicus)

❑ River Otter
(Lontra canadensis)

❑ Rock Vole
(Microtus chrotorrhinus)

❑ Short-tailed Shrew
(Blarina brevicauda)

❑ Silver-haired Bat
(Lasionycteris noctivagans)

❑ Small footed Bat
(Myotis leibii)

❑ Smokey Shrew
(Sorex fumeus)

❑ Snowshoe Hare
(Lepus americanus)

❑ Southern Flying
Squirrel
(Glaucomys volans)

❑ Striped Skunk
(Mephitis mephitis)

❑ Southern Bog
Lemming
(Synaptomys cooperi)

❑ Southern
Red-backed Vole
(Clethrionomys gapperi)

❑ Star-nosed Mole
(Condylura cristata)

❑ Water Shrew
(Sorex palustris)

❑ White-footed Mouse
(Peromyscus leucopus)

 **DAX FACTS**

White-tailed Deer. *Photograph ©2007 Gary VanRiper*

❑ White-tailed Deer
(Odocoileus virginianus)

❑ Woodchuck
(Marmota monax)

❑ Woodland
Jumping Mouse
(Napaeozapus insignis)

❑ Woodland Vole
(Microtus pinetorum)

Woodchuck.
Photograph ©2007 Gary VanRiper

About the Authors

Gary and Justin VanRiper are a father-and-son writing team residing in Camden, New York, with their family and cat, Dax. They spend many summer and autumn days at camp on Fourth Lake in the Adirondacks.

The Adirondack Kids® began as a short home writing exercise when Justin was in third grade. Encouraged after a public reading of an early draft at a Parents As Reading Partners (PARP) program in their school district, the project grew into a middle reader chapter book series.

The Adirondack Kids® #5 – *Islands in the Sky*, won the 2005–06 Adirondack Literary Award for Best Children's Book.

Justin and Gary VanRiper in the library of their Camden, NY home. *Photo by Carol VanRiper © 2006 Adirondack Kids Press*

About the Illustrators

Carol McCurn VanRiper lives and works in Camden, New York. She is also the wife and mother, respectively, of *The Adirondack Kids*® co-authors, Gary and Justin VanRiper. She inherited the job as publicist when *The Adirondack Kids*® grew from a family dream into a small company. Her black and white interior illustrations appear in *The Adirondack Kids*®, books #4 – #7.

Susan Loeffler is a freelance illustrator who lives and works in upstate New York.

Watch for more adventures
of The Adirondack Kids® *coming soon.*

The **Adirondack Kids**® #1

Justin Robert is ten years old and likes computers, biking and peanut butter cups. But his passion is animals. When an uncommon pair of Common Loons takes up residence on Fourth Lake near the family camp, he will do anything he can to protect them.

The **Adirondack Kids**® #2
Rescue on Bald Mountain

Justin Robert and Jackie Salsberry are on a special mission. It is Fourth of July weekend in the Adirondacks and time for the annual ping-pong ball drop at Inlet. Their best friend, Nick Barnes, has won the opportunity to release the balls from a seaplane, but there is just one problem. He is afraid of heights. With a single day remaining before the big event, Justin and Jackie decide there is only one way to help Nick overcome his fear. Climb Bald Mountain!

All on sale wherever great books on the Adirondacks are found.

The Adirondack Kids® #3
The Lost Lighthouse

Justin Robert, Jackie Salsberry and Nick Barnes are fishing under sunny Adirondack skies when a sudden and violent storm chases them off Fourth Lake and into an unfamiliar forest – a forest that has harbored a secret for more than 100 years.

The Adirondack Kids® #4
The Great Train Robbery

It's all aboard the train at the North Creek station, and word is out there are bandits in the region. Will the train be robbed? Justin Robert and Jackie Salsberry are excited. Nick Barnes is bored – but he won't be for long.

Also available on **The Adirondack Kids®** official web site
www.ADIRONDACKKIDS.com
Watch for more adventures of The Adirondack Kids® coming soon.

The Adirondack Kids® #5
Islands in the Sky

Justin Robert, Jackie Salsberry and Nick Barnes head for the Adirondack high peaks wilderness – while Justin's calico cat, Dax, embarks on an unexpected tour of the Adirondack Park.

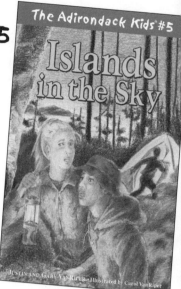

The Adirondack Kids® #6
Secret of the Skeleton Key

While preparing their pirate ship for the Anything That Floats Race, Justin and Nick discover an antique bottle riding the waves on Fourth Lake. Inside the bottle is a key that leads The Adirondack Kids to unlock an old camp mystery.

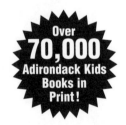

Over **70,000** Adirondack Kids Books in Print!

Also available on **The Adirondack Kids®** official web site
www.ADIRONDACKKIDS.com
Watch for more adventures of The Adirondack Kids® coming soon.